THE T

The
Treasure Hunt

J. M. Evans

DERNIER PUBLISHING
Tonbridge

Copyright © J.M. Evans 2005

First published 2005

Published by Dernier Publishing
P.O. Box 403, Tonbridge, TN9 9BJ, England
www.dernierpublishing.com

ISBN 0 9536963 1 6

Book design and production for the publisher by
Bookprint Creative Services, P.O. Box 827, BN21 3YJ, England.
Printed in Great Britain.

Contents

ONE
The Lorry

"Let's have another look at that clue," said Lance. He and Joel paused under a newly lit street-light, a mile or so from where the youth club treasure hunt had started. Joel handed the clue to Lance, who read it for what seemed like the hundredth time, hoping that more words would somehow mysteriously appear to guide him. "'Take the 007 turning'," sighed Lance. "That's all it says." His fair hair gleamed in the orange glow of the street-light as he looked round for inspiration.

"I wish we knew this part of town better," muttered Joel. Lance nodded in agreement. They were on the edge of the industrial estate, where warehouses and workshops took over from the rows of terraced houses. It all looked very grey and concrete, quiet now, although it was busy during the day.

The boys hesitated in the growing dusk. They had known each other for as long as they could remember, because their mums had been friends since before they had been born. They were about the same height, both tall for their twelve years, but different in appearance; Lance was slim and fair, Joel was more solidly built with dark hair that started to curl if he left it too long between haircuts.

"The 007 turning," repeated Joel slowly, then shook his head. "If it does mean James Bond, I can't see why. He'd never come to this boring place!"

Lance nodded and sighed. "Before this we were doing so well! We must have made a mistake somewhere. Maybe we didn't go north after the war memorial. Perhaps you were wrong."

"I was not wrong! We definitely went north!" protested Joel.

Lance was not persuaded. "So why haven't we seen anyone else from the youth club for the last ten minutes?"

"Maybe everyone else is wrong?" suggested Joel. Lance gave him a friendly punch.

"I don't think so!" he laughed. "You made a mistake and don't want to admit it!"

"No way!" laughed Joel, punching him back. "You just don't want to admit that I'm always right! But we'd better go back to the Club," he added. "It's getting dark and we've obviously lost the hunt. Someone's probably eaten the treasure by now."

"Eaten it?" asked Lance, grinning. "It could be a book – that wouldn't taste very nice!"

Joel gave him a withering look. "Prizes are always sweets or chocolate for this sort of thing, you know that. As it's nearly Easter, it might even be an Easter egg!"

"Well what if we just go down as far as that tile shop place," suggested Lance, indicating a bright red and yellow sign announcing "Tills Tiles" at the end of a row of warehouses a little further on. "007 might be on an advertisement or a phone number on one of the warehouses."

Joel sighed. "I suppose you might be right."

"After all, we don't want Debbie and Ravi beating us to the treasure, do we?"

"No way!" agreed Joel. Debbie was Joel's sister, a year older than the boys. Ravi was a newer friend, not long moved in to the area, but friend or no friend, this was a competition!

The atmosphere was getting darker and gloomier by the minute as Lance and Joel walked further into the deserted industrial estate. Shadows lengthened. A faint, acrid smell of oily tar hung in the evening air and the boys' footsteps echoed on the empty, unlit buildings as they looked around for the elusive 007.

"It's well creepy," whispered Joel, stopping in front of Tills Tiles.

Lance nodded, shivering slightly, not just with the cool of the evening. "There's nothing 007 here. Let's go."

"Unless he's hiding in that oasis," suggested Joel, grinning as he pointed out a group of dusty, tired-looking bushes which clung to life by the pavement in the concrete desert. Lance laughed aloud, his laugh echoing eerily round the buildings. The boys grinned at each other. Joel cupped his hands ready to hoot loudly, then stopped as the stillness was broken by the sound of an engine approaching very fast. A dirty white lorry was tearing up the road towards the boys, like a cat being chased by a dog. It thundered up to the entrance of Tills Tiles and screeched to a halt with a jolt, narrowly missing the boys, who stepped quickly back. With the engine still racing, a small, mean-looking man wearing a filthy boiler suit jumped out of the passenger side of the cab, slammed the door shut and ran to open the warehouse doors. Lance and Joel stared in shock.

Seeing them watching, the driver of the lorry, a thick-set white man with a scruffy beard, wound down his window. "Oi! What are you looking at?" he shouted roughly. The boys turned quickly away, but just as they did, a loud thumping and muffled shouting came from the back of the lorry. But there were no windows! Astonished, Joel and Lance both turned to look. "I said get out of here!" yelled the driver savagely at them, revving up the lorry's engine. He screeched into the warehouse as soon as the doors were open.

The boys turned and fled. Adding to their fright, a police car sped past them as they ran, lights flashing, its siren bursting through the quiet of the night. Lance and Joel continued to run long after they had left the industrial estate behind. "What do you make of that?" panted Joel eventually, doubling up over a garden wall to get his breath back.

"There's no way that lorry was doing under the speed limit!" declared Lance, hanging onto a telegraph pole and panting equally as loudly. "Or the police car!"

"Yeah! I've never been so scared in my life! And what do you think that thumping and shouting was inside the lorry?" asked Joel.

"Surely there can't have been anyone in there – they wouldn't be able to see out!"

"More to the point, how would they be able to breathe?" The boys looked at each other sombrely.

"No wonder whoever it was inside was banging and yelling," remarked Lance. "I would too, if I was shut in there by those awful men!"

"Me too!" agreed Joel. Suddenly realising the significance of what they had just seen, they stopped in their tracks and stared at each other in amazement. "Are you thinking what I'm thinking?" asked Joel.

Lance nodded slowly. "That police car was chasing the lorry. Do you think there really were people shut inside?"

Joel shrugged. "It sounded like it," he admitted. "But that's not a crime, is it?" And then he saw it. A little further ahead on the other side of the road. BOND ROAD. "Bond Road!" he yelled, grabbing Lance's arm.

"Our 007 turning!" groaned Lance. "I can't believe we missed it!"

TWO
Sharing the Story

Tina, the youth club leader, had given out all the prizes for the treasure hunt and was organising a search party for Joel and Lance by the time they arrived back at the youth club. With all the joking about them being last, they forgot about the white lorry for a while.

Much to their chagrin, Ravi and Debbie had won first prize. "The treasure was great!" enthused Ravi, as the four walked down the road to his house. The four of them always went there after youth club, because their mums got together to chat and pray.

"A whole box of chocolates all to ourselves!" gloated Debbie. "Delicious!" She and Ravi grinned at each other and rubbed their stomachs.

"You haven't eaten them all already!" gasped Joel in horror. "You greedy pigs! You could have saved some for us!"

"How dare you call us pigs?" gasped Debbie, pulling the shiny purple box of goodies out of her bag.

"Whoops!" said Joel sheepishly, seeing the treasure appear. Lance and Ravi laughed.

Debbie glared at her brother. "We were only joking about eating them all. Actually, we thought we would

15

share them, but you're not having any, Joel, unless you apologise for calling me a pig!" Her dark, curly hair bounced around her shoulders, as it always did when she was cross.

"Sorry, sorry, sorry," said Joel immediately, his eyes on the chocolates. "But," he added, "actually, if you had eaten them all, you would have been pigs!" He did a snorting pig impression, which was so funny they all laughed, even Debbie.

It wasn't long before they were sipping lemonade in Ravi's bedroom, keeping the chocolates away from Willow, Ravi's little black dog. She had been known to polish off a whole box before now, clawing her way into the wrappers!

"So what took you so long on the treasure hunt?" Debbie asked Joel and Lance a little later, sinking into a bean-bag.

"We missed Bond Road," admitted Lance. "We walked right down to the industrial estate, looking for 007!" They all laughed.

"Talking too much I expect," said Ravi, unwrapping a vanilla fudge for an ecstatic Willow before offering the sweets to his friends.

"Bet you didn't see him!" grinned Debbie, choosing a strawberry cream.

"No, but we did see something else," remembered Lance, suddenly serious. Between them, he and Joel told their story of the dirty white lorry by the tile warehouse, the mean-looking man who had opened the doors, the surly driver, the thumping and shouting that had come from the back of the lorry and the police car that had sped past.

"Perhaps we ought to phone the police," said Lance, when their tale ended.

"Just because you saw a lorry speeding?" laughed Ravi, sipping his lemonade. "You can't do that!"

"We haven't got much to go on," Lance admitted.

"Maybe you just imagined the thumping and shouting," suggested Debbie.

"No, we definitely didn't," said Joel.

"There must be some logical explanation," said Ravi. "No, Willow, no more sweets, they're bad for you. The banging could have been boxes or crates falling over in the lorry – you know, you said the driver stopped suddenly . . ." Lance and Joel shook their heads.

"It was definitely people," said Lance, his mouth full of toffee whirl.

Joel nodded in agreement. "Boxes and crates don't shout!" he pointed out. There was a short silence as the four minds got to work.

"I've got it!" said Debbie. "There was a third person, a work mate or something, maybe more than one, and there wasn't room in the front of the lorry, so they just got in the back!"

"I suppose it could have been," admitted Joel slowly. "But it wasn't that sort of lorry – not like a workman's van."

"And the banging was really fierce. It didn't seem like a friendly shout," added Lance. "It was more . . . angry, or frightened. Don't you think, Joel?"

"Yeah," nodded Joel. "Which is exactly what you would be if you were shut in there, especially with that maniac driver. It would frighten you to death. And anyway, what about the police car?"

"Coincidence?" shrugged Ravi. "Going to a break-in or something?"

"Well, there's no point worrying about it now," said Debbie. "It's not our problem. Anyone for another chocolate?"

"But don't you think we ought to do something?" objected Lance. "Someone might have been trying to get our attention, let us know they were imprisoned in the back of that lorry!"

"I really don't think . . ." began Debbie, but at that moment, Ravi's mum called that it was time to go home.

"I'll keep the rest of the chocolates for next week," promised Debbie.

"And we'll decide what to do about the lorry at school tomorrow," said Ravi, collecting the lemonade glasses.

"That would be good," agreed Lance. Debbie and Joel nodded too.

"See you all at lunch time, then?" said Ravi. "Meet by the water fountain?"

"OK," said Lance. "Let's hope it's not too late!"

On the walk back to their flat, Lance started to tell his

mum about the treasure hunt and the lorry, but it was only five minutes' walk and he hadn't managed to say much before they were home. Lance had to go straight to bed when they got in; as his mum pointed out, it was late and he could tell her about everything after school tomorrow.

Lance opened his mouth to object, but his mum looked tired so he decided to leave it. It hadn't been easy for her since his dad had left a couple of years ago and it was no use arguing with her, it would just put her in a bad mood. But as he got ready for bed, Lance couldn't get his mind off the lorry, the shouting and knocking, the driver who had yelled at them. It bothered him. Perhaps he should have got his mum to phone the police. He couldn't just say it wasn't his problem, as Debbie had. To be fair, she hadn't been there, she couldn't understand . . . but there was definitely something not right about it. "So what should I do?" he asked himself, as he absentmindedly looked at the bible verse for the day on his calendar. It hit him like a football in the stomach. "Do for others what you would like them to do for you," he read. "Luke 6:31."

"That's it!" he whispered to himself, feeling a tingling run down his spine. "If it was me shut in that lorry, I'd want someone to help. And maybe nobody else knows – only me and Joel." That was an awesome thought.

Lance always prayed before he went to bed, but mostly it was just a quick thank you for the day, without really thinking too much about it. This time he could feel the seriousness of what he was saying. He could even feel the powerful presence of God with him as he prayed. "Dear Lord, if you want me to, please help me to help the people in the lorry. In Jesus' name, Amen." As he got into bed, he knew that God had answered. The answer was "I will".

THREE

Plan and Action

Joel and Debbie got a lift to school in the mornings, but Ravi and Lance walked together. The morning after the treasure hunt, it wasn't long before the subject of the lorry came up. "Honestly, Rav, I think it's something serious," Lance told him.

"Don't worry, I believe you," said Ravi. "I mean, from what you said yesterday, it didn't sound normal."

"I prayed about it last night," said Lance. "I just had to. I've never done that before. I mean, I've prayed about stuff, of course I have, but this was, I don't know, different."

"I know what you mean," said Ravi straight away. "That happened to me when my mum was ill before Christmas, remember? We'd not long moved here. She had to go to hospital."

"I remember that. She nearly died."

"I prayed then. Really prayed."

Lance grinned at him. "That's exactly how I felt last night! And then I knew God had answered me!"

"Me too!" said Ravi eagerly. "I just knew Mum would get better. Dad knew too, at the same time. He'd been fasting, but after that we went out for a pizza!"

"And she did get better, didn't she?"

"Even the doctors said it was a miracle!"

"Well we need another one now!" said Lance, his eyes shining. "I prayed that God would help me to help the people in the back of the lorry."

"Wow! You mean you've got to do something yourself?"

"Well yes, but I was hoping you'd help too – you and Joel and Debbie, if they want to."

"Are you kidding? Of course we will! Well I certainly will, and I can't imagine them letting you and me have all the fun without them. Wow, a real mystery to solve!"

* * *

"But we're just kids," Joel objected later, when the four of them discussed the problem at lunch-time, grouped around the fountain. "What can we do?"

"Children are just as important as adults," said Lance.

"Why should God only give things to adults to do?" agreed Ravi.

"OK, OK," said Joel, "I know all that, but what I'm saying is, what can we *do*?"

Debbie pursed her lips. "Do you honestly think we should do anything? I mean, it could be dangerous." There was a short silence.

"I just know somehow, that the Lord wants me, wants us, to do something," said Lance slowly. "I can't explain it, but . . . I just think we should. And if it's God's will, then he'll protect us."

"OK then," agreed Debbie. "In that case, we ought to pray about it."

"Now?" asked Joel. "Right here?" He looked round at the groups of people laughing, talking and playing football.

"Debbie's right. Let's just do it quickly," said Lance, closing his eyes. "Lord, if you want us to do anything, please help us to know what to do and be obedient to you. Amen."

"Amen," agreed the others and they looked round at each other in eager anticipation.

"So what's the plan then?" asked Joel.

"Well, maybe we could go down to the warehouses again tonight and have a proper look round," said Lance. "See if the lorry's there, see if there's anyone inside . . . see if there's anything odd-looking . . ." The four nodded to each other.

"I'm in!" said Ravi.

"I think Mum will let us," said Debbie, "as it's Friday."

"Shall we meet by the war memorial then?" suggested Lance. "It's straight down from there. Seven o'clock all right? It won't be dark then, but hopefully everyone working at the tile warehouse and the other places will have gone home."

"Good plan," agreed Joel.

"I'll bring Willow," said Ravi eagerly. "She'll be good protection against crooks!"

"And everyone bring their mobile phones," said

Debbie. "Just in case. I know the Lord will look after us, but we should still be sensible." The four grinned at each other as the bell went for afternoon registration. This had got to better than a youth club treasure hunt – this was going to be a real, spine-tingling adventure!

"All right!" said Lance, his eyes shining. "Until tonight then!"

* * *

The walk down to the industrial estate was cheerful. Debbie had thought to take the chocolates, Willow was her usual cute self, the evening was warm and all four were full of bravado. But as Joel pointed out the sign for Tills Tiles, the little group began to walk slower. Although it was still quite light, the area somehow held an aura of darkness about it and everything was quiet and still, almost as if it were holding its breath, waiting for something to happen.

"What are we going to do when we get there?" asked Debbie, checking behind to make sure nobody was following them.

"We'll start by looking in the window of the tile place, as if we were interested in tiles," replied Lance. "If we see anyone watching us, we'll talk about bathrooms or kitchens."

"That'll be interesting," grinned Joel and the boys all laughed. Debbie didn't.

"It's not funny, you know," she said. "This isn't an outing, it's like, real." The others nodded sheepishly. "It could be dangerous," she added.

"How about posting a guard?" suggested Ravi. "I'll do that if you like. Keep an eye out for lorries coming or anything suspicious. I've got Willow for company."

"Good idea," said Lance. "If you stand by those bushes, you can see the traffic both ways." Everyone nodded agreement, so leaving Ravi on the pavement, the others walked across the bare concrete forecourt and looked in the door and window of the tile shop, their footsteps echoing harshly on the buildings. The sound of an engine approaching made them turn quickly round, but Ravi gave them the thumbs up and a few seconds later a blue van drove straight on by.

It was dark inside the shop and there didn't appear to be anybody there, or anything unusual. A cash desk stood to the left of the window and on the right was a closed door. "That goes to the warehouse bit, where the lorry went in," observed Lance. Apart from that, there were just rows and rows of displays of tiles of every colour, size and style imaginable.

"I thought tiles were tiles," remarked Debbie. "Look at all these!"

"I'm glad we haven't got tiles like that in our kitchen," observed Joel, pointing out the "Manager's Offer of the Week" on a display near the door; brown tiles with pictures of wrinkled vegetables.

"Disgusting," agreed Debbie, curling her lip. "No wonder the manager wants to get rid of them!"

Joel laughed. "I wouldn't even want to look at them while I was working here!"

Lance nodded too. "Well there's nothing here," he said. "Let's walk along a bit." There were four warehouses in the row, each with a shop-type door and window next to tall warehouse doors, high enough for lorries to get in. Disappointingly, there was absolutely nothing of interest to see at all. Everything was closed up and silent and if there were any secrets, there didn't seem to be any way of finding them out.

They went back to Ravi, who was waiting patiently with Willow. "See anything suspicious?" he asked, but he knew from their expressions that they hadn't. "How about looking round the back?" he suggested. There was a moment's silence. Out here in the front there was a road with street lights. Round the back . . . well, what might be round the back? "I think we should," said Ravi firmly. "We can't get this far then not do everything we can."

"We'll all go together then," nodded Lance. Debbie opened her mouth to speak, but no words came out, for just at that moment the sound of a lorry approaching made them all turn towards the road. "Oh no!" yelled Lance, as the white lorry came into view. "Run!" But in their panic the boys ran into each other; only Debbie made it safely behind the bushes near the pavement, panting and frightened.

FOUR

Threatened!

The driver of the lorry stopped, seeing the boys blocking his way to the warehouse. He jumped down from the lorry. It was the same driver as last night. Willow growled deep in her throat.

"You again!" said the man incredulously and rather angrily, ignoring Willow and looking at Joel and Lance. "With a Paki friend, I see. Teaching you tricks, is he?" There was a shocked silence from the boys. "Well, speak up for yourselves, what are you doing here?" the man shouted roughly. Willow started to bark furiously, but although Ravi held tight to her lead, he didn't try to stop her. Faced with the aggressive man, the boys couldn't think of an answer.

"Umm," began Lance. The man sneered at the dog, walked right up close to the boys and stood over them with his arms folded. He was so close they could smell the sweat and filth on his blue, stained boiler-suit.

"Well?" he said quietly, menacingly.

"We were just . . . looking at the tiles," managed Lance eventually. Joel nodded.

"My friends thought they heard somebody in your lorry last night," said Ravi boldly, looking the man in the eye.

"Is that right?" The boys all swallowed hard as the man turned his gaze to Ravi. His beard bristled and his face got redder and angrier and contorted into a horribly menacing grimace. Lance stepped back and his heart nearly missed a beat as out of the corner of his eye he saw Debbie creeping up to the back of the lorry. What is she up to? he thought in horror. The driver's back was to her, but there was another man in the lorry; the one who had opened the warehouse doors last night. "Oh God, don't let them see her!" he silently prayed.

"If I ever catch you anywhere near here again, I'll lock you up in the dark and you'll never see daylight again!" snarled the man, so suddenly and ferociously that the boys all jumped back. Out of the corner of his eye, Lance saw Debbie half creep, half run back to her hiding place behind the bushes.

"Just get out!" yelled the man. Ravi started to run towards home, Willow dragging at the lead, still barking fit to bust, but Joel and Lance ran towards the bushes.

"Where are you going?" hissed Ravi, but he didn't need an answer, because there was Debbie, crouching, hidden behind the greenery. They all ducked down and the boys breathed deeply.

"If that was an adventure, I don't like them!" said Joel, gasping for breath. "I didn't know men like that existed in real life!"

When the noise of the lorry's engine had faded in the warehouse and the doors slammed shut, they all breathed properly again. "Can you believe . . ." began Lance indignantly, but Debbie interrupted him.

"There were definitely people in that lorry," she informed them excitedly, her eyes shining with her discovery. "Did you see me? I knocked on the back. I have never been so scared in my life! And someone knocked back, just gently, like they were afraid of being heard, but there were definitely, *definitely* people in there! I heard them talking too, though it was muffled and I didn't hang about. I was so scared that man was going to turn round and see me!"

"Well done Debbie," said Lance, clapping her on the back.

"That was so brave," added Ravi and Joel nodded his agreement.

"I was afraid the other man might see you though," added Joel.

"What other man?" asked Debbie quickly. "I didn't see another man!"

"He was in the cab. With mirrors to see out the back." Debbie gasped and turned pale.

"I can't believe I just did that!" she said, shaking her head in disbelief at her close escape.

"Well, you did and we're all here and we're all safe," said Lance firmly. "We prayed for protection, and so far, the Lord has protected us, as we knew he would. And well done for speaking up, Ravi, that was brave too."

"Yeah, after he called you a Paki!" said Joel. "And more

or less said you were a thief!"

"He said what?" asked Debbie incredulously. "I can't believe it! Some people are so . . . ignorant!"

Ravi shrugged. "It doesn't matter, don't worry about it. Willow didn't like the man though; she'd have bitten him if I'd let her! But anyway, now we have to decide what to do next."

"Go home!" said Joel firmly. "That's enough excitement for one night! I don't mind saying, I nearly had a heart attack when I saw Debbie at the back of the lorry. And that gross, horrible, disgusting man – he stank! And his breath – ugh, I want to have a shower!"

As he was speaking, the lorry emerged once more from the warehouse. "It's our lorry," whispered Ravi, motioning to them all to stay out of sight, "going back the way it came." When the noise of the engine had faded into the distance, there was a short silence.

"They weren't there long," observed Debbie.

"Do you think they were dropping the people off?" wondered Ravi.

"They may have been kidnapped," suggested Lance. Joel pursed his lips.

"Not kidnapped, not two days in a row, surely?"

"Perhaps they're illegal immigrants," suggested Debbie.

"Could be," said Lance. "But in that case, you'd think they'd keep quiet in the back of the lorry, not knock to let us know they're there."

"That's true," admitted Debbie.

"It's no good just wondering," said Ravi. "We need something definite to go on. We ought to look round the back now, see if we can get any clues."

"Wouldn't it be trespassing?" asked Debbie. "I don't think we ought to."

"Let's just get on with it," said Joel. "If we're quick, we'll have time to go to the park before we go home. We told Mum we were walking Willow with Ravi – she sort of assumed we were going to the park."

"What do you think, Lance?" asked Ravi.

"We ought to pray again," he replied. "We need to know what to do and we know God answers our prayers."

The others nodded. "OK, let's go for it!" said Ravi, closing his eyes. They clustered round on the pavement with the dog. "Please, dear Lord, show us what to do," prayed Ravi. "Amen. Your turn, Debbie."

"Dear Father, we do pray you would keep the people in the lorry safe," prayed Debbie. "And if they're scared, please give them your peace." Joel was next.

"Um, I don't know what to say, God," stuttered Joel, "But if there's a problem, we pray that you would sort it out . . . or help us sort it out. Amen."

"Go on, Lance," urged Joel, after a short pause.

"Dear Lord," began Lance, his tone serious. "I don't understand why you sent us here, except that it seems important. We ask in Jesus' name that you would lead the way. And we pray against the work of the enemy, Amen." They all opened their eyes.

"Wow, where did you get that last bit about the enemy?" asked Joel.

Lance shrugged. "It seemed relevant. I've heard people pray it before. So, do we look round the back now or not?" he asked his friends.

"Let's just do it," sighed Joel. "Get it over with."

Ravi nodded agreement. "I think Joel's right. Better look in the shop again too. With us, Debbie?"

Debbie shrugged. "Couldn't we . . ."

"Yes or no?" interrupted Joel.

"Yes!" said Debbie, looking surprised at herself for her reply.

After checking the shop, which looked just the same as before, the little group followed the high, bare brick wall round to the back of the warehouse, trying not to make too much noise with their feet. The silence was broken by a bird singing cheerfully, which sounded odd amongst the bare, drab, man-made surroundings. "Look out for CCTV cameras!" said Joel suddenly. The others stopped short. "No, it's OK," he assured them after a swift perusal of the back of the premises.

Debbie stopped. "Are you sure we should be doing this?" she asked.

"There's nothing to say it's private property," shrugged Joel. "Anyone can walk here. I just don't want those men recording us on cameras!" That wasn't a very nice thought. They all stood and looked round without getting too close, just in case. It seemed even darker round the back.

The whole area had a run-down look, dingy and dirty, with oil stains on the cracked concrete, rubbish flapping about and stacks of pallets in higgledy-piggledy heaps. A rusting yellow skip stood in the farthest corner and a large wire crate was overflowing with broken cardboard boxes. A fire door led to the back of the tile shop, but there was no other way in or out — even a couple of small windows high up had been boarded over.

"Absolutely nothing," said Lance.

"Well that's that then," said Joel. "To the park?" Suddenly, Willow started to bark up at the little windows.

"Willow's heard something!" yelled Ravi. They all ran to the wall to listen.

"It's nothing," said Debbie, after a minute's silence.

"Maybe it was a rat!" grinned Joel, making his fingers into ears above Debbie's head. "A big, fat rat!" And then he stopped. The four looked round at each other in horror and amazement. There was no mistaking it. From somewhere inside the building came the sound of a baby's cry, quickly hushed.

FIVE

Now What?

Debbie and Joel, Ravi and Willow were already on the swings at the park next day when Lance came running up. "Sorry I'm late," panted Lance. "Mum wouldn't let me go until I'd emptied all the bins and taken the dustbin round. Hello Willow," he added, patting the little black dog who had jumped off Ravi's lap to greet him, wagging her tail fit to bust, always pleased to have more company.

"No problem," said Ravi. "Me and Willow have only just got here too."

"That's OK then!" said Lance cheerfully. "So where's the best place to have a discussion? I couldn't sleep, thinking about what we're going to do next!"

"Better walk round the park," said Ravi, "or Willow will get bored."

"Me too!" agreed Joel, jumping off the swing and setting off. "Oh, and Mum sent us all a chocolate bar each. It's a peace offering."

"A what?" asked Lance, staring quizzically at the chocolate.

"Bad news, I'm afraid," admitted Debbie. She and Joel exchanged a glum look. "Me and Joel told Mum and Dad about last night – they wanted to know where we'd been and I felt we ought to tell the truth. They've forbidden us to go to the industrial estate again."

"Oh," said Lance. "Oh. That's a shame." His cheerful mood fell. This was a serious blow.

"I suppose you told them about the man?" guessed Ravi. Debbie and Joel nodded.

"You must admit," said Debbie, "it was awful what he said. About us never seeing daylight again!"

"Debbie told them that," said Joel, with a sigh.

"Well they asked what he said," retorted Debbie defensively. "And if the Lord wants us to do something, he's not going to want us to lie, is he?" The others shook their heads. However annoying it was, Debbie was absolutely right.

"Did you tell them about the baby crying?" asked Ravi.

"They said it probably came from a nearby house," replied Debbie, "because nobody replied when we shouted up."

"Well it didn't come from a house!" said Lance. "That's for sure!"

"We thought we'd better not argue," said Joel. "We were lucky to get away without being completely grounded!"

"And that was only because we told Mum and Dad that we prayed together about it all," added Debbie. "Then they promised to pray about it too." There was a silence as the four walked on round the park in the warm spring sunshine.

"You must admit, Lance, it's just what you'd expect from parents," said Ravi, trying to console his friend.

Lance nodded slowly, nibbling his chocolate bar. "That man was really scary, wasn't he, but he just wanted to get rid of us. I don't think he really meant what he said, do you?"

Debbie shrugged. "You never know with people like that."

"He might have locked us up in the warehouse with those other people!" said Joel with feeling. "That's if he didn't explode with anger first!"

"And what about my Willow?" gasped Ravi, bending down to hug his little dog and getting a lick on the face in return. "What might he do to her?" They all looked round at each other. That was not a nice thought!

Lance suddenly groaned. "This is getting us nowhere. We're just frightening ourselves for nothing. We don't even know those people are locked up – maybe that's why they didn't answer when we called. And what can we do now anyway?" he added gloomily, kicking a stone along the path.

"You and Ravi will just have to carry on without us," said Joel. "It's the only way. Just my luck to miss all the fun!"

Ravi nodded. "We could you know, Lance."

"'Til their parents tell ours!" sighed Lance. "That'll be at church tomorrow, if not before. Maybe I made a mistake about it all."

"Our one chance for a real adventure and now it's over!" complained Debbie. "Just when things were getting exciting!"

"Yeah," added Joel with a sigh. "The lorry, police car, the people in the back, those men, who are probably criminals . . ."

"And that baby," added Debbie, "crying from nowhere!"

Joel sighed again. "Our own real-life mystery and now we're never going to solve it!" There was a gloomy pause, but Lance looked thoughtfully round at his friends.

"If it is what we think it is, if we really think that people were locked in the back of the lorry, maybe kidnapped, and if a baby is really being kept in that warehouse, then it's not really exciting in that sort of way. If you see what I mean," he added after a pause.

"You're right," nodded Debbie, more sombrely. "I haven't been able to stop thinking about that baby in that horrid warehouse. Dreadful place for a baby."

"Perhaps there are more children, too," added Ravi. "Maybe they're all children!" There was a short silence as the severity of the situation sunk in.

"We've just got to do something!" said Lance at last. The others all nodded.

"If God wants you to, you'll have to carry on," said Debbie. "I don't think you made a mistake, Lance, I really don't."

"Me neither," agreed Ravi.

"Maybe we could do some research," suggested Joel. "We can go back to our house, we can do a search for kidnapped people on the internet, look up the news pages . . . we can all work together."

"That's a great idea!" nodded Lance more cheerfully.

"Maybe we could trace the lorry as well?" suggested Debbie. "It didn't have any writing on it, did it? Like the name of the company or anything like that?"

"No," said Joel straight away. "Nothing at all. I did notice that the number plate had the letters YOB at the end though. It seemed sort of fitting somehow."

"Well spotted, Joel!" said Lance, feeling better by the minute. "I didn't even think to look."

"OK then!" said Ravi, pausing in front of a board by the café advertising ice-creams. "Have we got time for ice-creams, or shall we go and get straight on?"

"Ice-cream sounds cool to me!" said Joel. "Cold, actually!"

The others groaned.

"I've got some money," said Lance, searching through his pockets for his wallet. "Getting an ice-cream won't take a minute!" Suddenly Joel froze.

"Forget the ice-cream!" he hissed. "Whatever you do, *don't turn round!*"

SIX

More Surprises

"Look at the ice-cream board, just keep looking at the board," begged Joel urgently.

"Why?" asked Lance, staring fixedly at the pictures of ice-creams without really seeing any of them.

"What is it?" asked Debbie, itching to turn round. "What's happening? Tell me now, Joel. This isn't one of your wind-ups, is it?"

"It's the driver of the lorry!" gasped Ravi, looking quickly round. "Now what?"

"Walk to the swings as if nothing's happened," said Joel. "Keep your backs to the car park, he's walking towards the café."

"Don't attract his attention, don't run," urged Debbie, desperate to get away as fast as her legs would carry her.

"He'll recognise Willow!" said Ravi, quickly picking up his little dog. They all ran the last few paces to the swings and sat down with their backs to the car park and café. Fortunately nobody else was around.

"Did he see us?" asked Debbie, in a slightly panicky voice.

"You look round, Debs, you're the only one he won't recognise," urged Lance. Debbie swallowed hard and stared at the café entrance.

"Don't stare like that!" spluttered Joel. "He'll see you looking!"

"Sit on your swing facing the opposite way," advised Ravi. "People do that, it won't look odd," he added as she hesitated. There was a brief silence while they all waited, hardly daring to breathe.

"I can't see him. He must have gone in the café," said Debbie at last and everyone let out a deep sigh of relief.

"Wow, that was close!" breathed Joel.

"No kidding! I can't believe this!" said Lance.

"You know, this is more than coincidence," said Ravi. "This has got to be God at work." The others nodded, wide-eyed and serious.

"So," said Lance, "shall we check out the car park first, see if the lorry's there?"

"If anyone's shut in it, maybe we can let them out!" agreed Joel.

"Good plan," nodded Lance. "We'll sneak up to the café first, make sure the man is definitely there. Then Debbie can go in, sit nearby and watch him, and text us if he leaves. OK, Debbie?"

"On my own?" she gasped. "I don't think so!"

"There's no choice!" argued Joel. "He knows what the rest of us look like!"

"I've got a hood, I can sit with my back to him," suggested Ravi. The others nodded.

"OK then," agreed Lance. "Me and Joel will check the

MORE SURPRISES   43

car park, with Willow, out of sight of the café, then if
there's time, we'll walk her round the park again a bit,
blend in. Is that OK with everyone?"

"What if he recognises Ravi?" asked Debbie dubiously.

"He can't do anything to us in the café!" grinned Ravi.
"Even if we walked right up to him and said hello!"
Everyone grinned; even Debbie managed a smile.
Although it was a bit scary, it was good to be back on track
again.

"Text us, let us know straight away if he's not there,"
urged Lance. "Try not to let him recognise you. We don't
want him following us home!"

"We certainly don't!" gasped Debbie.

"And you let us know about the lorry," said Ravi as he
pulled his hood up over his head, handed Willow's lead
to Lance and ushered Debbie quickly towards the café
before she could change her mind. "Back in a minute,
Willow, be good!"

* * *

Going the long way round to keep out of sight of the café,
Joel and Lance made their way to the car park. "It's
there!" yelled Joel excitedly, seeing the white lorry half-
hidden by bushes and trees.

"The yob-lorry!" grinned Lance.

"So, do we just walk up and knock on the back?" asked
Joel.

"Maybe we could pretend to be looking for something near it," suggested Lance. Joel grinned.

"Well I'm sure I left my football here somewhere," he said loudly, as a couple with a baby in a buggy passed by. "Look in the bushes," he said in a low voice to Lance.

"I think it was more this way, actually," said Lance, grinning at his friend, edging slowly towards the lorry.

"Perhaps it's stuck in these bushes," said Joel, getting even nearer. Willow looked up at them quizzically. "Look for the ball, Willow," urged Joel and she immediately started sniffing in the undergrowth. "Willow makes a great undercover agent!" admired Joel. Lance laughed. Once behind the lorry, both boys stopped and stood still.

"Hear anything?" whispered Lance. Both boys listened intently. Joel shook his head, then jumped in alarm as Willow barked, nearly tore the lead from his grasp and a hand gripped his shoulder.

"Got any money?" asked a familiar voice. "Hi Willow, don't knock me over, I'm going again in a minute!" It was Ravi!

"Oh, Ravi, don't do that!" gasped Joel. "You nearly frightened me to death, creeping up like that!"

"Sorry," grinned Ravi. "I see you've found the lorry. The driver's in the café, on his own. I can't stop, Debbie's waiting in the queue, but everything in there's really expensive, even just for a coke. We need more money. Have either of you got some we can borrow?"

"Take my wallet," said Lance, then seeing a lady

walking past he added, "We're just looking for our ball."
Ravi gave him an odd look.

"Your ball?" he asked, surprised, then suddenly the
penny dropped. "Oh right, your ball," he nodded
conspiratorially. "Let me know if you find it!"

*   *   *

"You've been ages," muttered Debbie crossly, taking the
wallet from Ravi, who arrived just in time to pay for the
drinks, his hood well over his face. "Hurry up, that table's
free over there." She pointed out an empty table behind
the lorry driver, who was reading a newspaper while
tucking in to a late breakfast of sausages, bacon, eggs and
beans. As they passed, the man wiped ketchup from his
beard with the back of his hand. Debbie and Ravi
grimaced at each other. "Ugh, that is so sick," muttered
Debbie as she placed their cokes on the table behind him.
"I'm glad I'm not eating anything, that would really put
me off!" Ravi grinned and pulled his hood down.

"I'll sit here," he said, taking the chair immediately
behind the man. "Let me know if I need this back up," he
added, indicating his hood. Debbie nodded and sat
opposite him. From there she had a good view of the back
of the man; his leather jacket, greasy hair and bald patch.

"I kept watching this table while I was in the queue,"
whispered Debbie once they were settled. "I'm glad it's still
free. He can't see us here unless he turns right round. And

I hope this isn't a waste of money," she added, counting up the small amount of change ruefully.

Ravi grinned as he sipped his coke through a straw. "It's Lance's money anyway!" he laughed. Just at that moment the man's mobile phone rang. The friends sat still and strained their ears to listen through the clatter of the café.

"You're always late!" they heard the man say rather roughly, then there was a pause. "Five minutes then, and if you're not here by then, I'm coming round." He growled something they couldn't hear, then snapped his phone shut with a harsh click.

"He's meeting someone here!" said Ravi in a low voice. Debbie nodded.

"I'll text Joel and Lance," she whispered, "tell them to watch in the car park for people coming." Ravi nodded.

"Tell them to get registration numbers too. Tell them we'll stay here and listen to what the meeting's about." Debbie nodded, her eyes shining with the secret.

"Good work," said Ravi when she'd sent the message. "Nice coke," he added, as someone walked past the table.

Suddenly the driver stood up, scraping his chair on the floor. "Hood!" hissed Debbie urgently. Ravi was quick, but the man turned round and stared at him. Ravi could feel the gaze burning through the fabric of his hood.

SEVEN
The Meeting

The friends frantically sipped coke until they were certain the driver had turned away. The normality of the café seemed unreal, almost like another world. Debbie was panic-stricken. "Do you think he recognised you?" she asked, watching the man out of the corner of her eye as he approached the counter.

"I don't know," replied Ravi, swallowing hard. "I didn't dare look up. Where is he now? What's he doing? Do you think we should go?"

"I think we should stay," said Debbie firmly, ignoring the sinking feeling in her stomach. "He's just getting more ketchup," she added, her heart beginning to pound less fiercely. "Maybe he just stared because you startled him, putting your hood up so quick. Anyway, remember what you said outside, that he can't do anything to us in here? We need to know what the meeting's about."

"OK," nodded Ravi.

"Then do you want to get a boat out on the lake?" Debbie asked suddenly, kicking Ravi's ankle.

"Ow! No," replied Ravi, looking totally amazed. "Why?"

"Because," Debbie hissed, "the man's coming back and

we're trying to look like two normal people in a café!"

"Oh!" said Ravi rather sheepishly. Then in a louder voice, "A boat on the lake. Good idea. We'll ask the others." At that, Ravi heard a chair scrape behind him and felt the driver's presence. "Did he stare again?" he mouthed anxiously.

Debbie shook her head. "Not exactly stare, he did look, but not exactly at us, he looked, like, all round. I think we're OK."

"It's making me feel on edge, sitting with my back to him, not being able to see what he's doing," whispered Ravi. "For all I know he could have a knife in his hand."

"He has!" said Debbie. Ravi whirled round immediately, but seeing nothing untoward, turned back.

"What did you say that for?" he asked rather crossly. "I thought I was about to be stabbed!"

"He's got a knife . . . and fork!" explained Debbie, grinning. Ravi grimaced.

"Ha ha, very funny!"

Debbie's gaze fixed suddenly on the door. "Don't look round," she whispered, "but the man's just nodded to someone coming in the café." Ravi nodded and leaned forward so Debbie could keep her voice low. The meeting was about to take place!

"What's he like?" whispered Ravi.

"Looks Chinese or something like that. Smart, wearing a suit," she added quietly. "Looks like a business man, with a black briefcase. He's going to the counter." Hearing her mobile bleep, she got it out of her pocket and read the message. "Lance says, the lorry's empty, do they need to keep looking for the person? I'll tell them it's the smart Chinese man."

Ravi nodded. "Perhaps he's the boss." As Debbie sent the message, Ravi heard another chair being moved behind him and the clatter as a cup and saucer were placed on the table. The hair on the back of his neck prickled as he heard the two men greet each other, one gruffly, the other most politely.

"I'm sick of you being late!" grumbled the lorry driver. "It's the same every time."

"And a very pleasant good morning to you too," said the new man, with a slight foreign accent. "You British have such a terrible fascination with time and sadly, your tea is really quite atrocious. However, business is good, so we won't let that bother us, will we?"

"Don't mock me, I haven't got time for messing about," snarled the driver. "Where's what I came for?"

"Patience, dear boy, patience," said the new man calmly, stirring his tea. "I have it safely on my person. But first of all, there are some small business matters we need to discuss. Everything is going to plan, I trust?" The driver gave a disgruntled humph and started to speak. Unfortunately, just at that moment a small child nearby started to kick and scream.

"I don't want it!" wailed the little girl, at full volume.

"That's annoying," said Debbie, with a black look

towards the child and her parents. Ravi nodded.

"Keep watching though. He's going to give him something, sounded like. See if you can see what it is." Pretending to fiddle with her shoes, Debbie carefully shifted her chair a little so that she could see the new man a bit better. After a couple of frustrating minutes, while Debbie and Ravi could hear nothing of the conversation going on at the next table, the child was eventually pacified and calm returned to the café just as the second man was taking a large brown envelope from his briefcase.

". . . rest assured, prices are continuing to rise," he was saying genially. Then to Debbie's alarm his face changed, his voice lowered to a hiss and he leaned across the table with a hard, cruel stare which made her think of a snake about to strike its prey. "But you had better make sure that you show me respect. We don't want anything nasty to happen to you now, do we?" Ravi and Debbie stared at each other in consternation as the man abruptly handed the driver the envelope, picked up his briefcase and left.

"Has he gone?" asked Ravi. Debbie nodded.

"I'll never complain about our teachers ever again," she whispered fervently, then turned her attention back to the driver. "He's opening a big envelope the man gave him."

"What's in it?"

"Can't see," said Debbie, craning round the table. "Let's go now!" she whispered suddenly, grabbing her phone and Lance's wallet from the table. "You get out quick with your hood up. I'll look as we pass." As she reached the man's table, Debbie dropped the wallet. "Whoops!" she said with a smile in the driver's direction. Bending down to pick it up, she took a good look at the contents of the envelope.

"I saw what's in the envelope!" said Debbie, panting with excitement as she caught up with Ravi on the café steps.

"Shh!" panicked Ravi, looking round quickly in case the driver was following them or the man in the suit was still around. Nobody had heard, but Lance and Joel were waving to them from the swings.

"Tell us in a minute!" said Ravi, clapping Debbie on the back as they ran to join their friends. "Wow, can you believe what happened in there? You did great!"

"Anything to report?" asked Lance as soon as they were together again and Willow had got over the excitement of her reunion with Ravi.

"No kidding!" said Debbie excitedly.

EIGHT

More Information

Debbie grinned triumphantly. "The new man with the briefcase gave the lorry driver a big envelope and it had passports in it!" The others stared open-mouthed and wide-eyed at this information. "I got to see by dropping your wallet, Lance. I had a good look while I was picking it up. He tried to hide them with his newspaper, but I'm sure they were passports!" Flushed with success, she leaned back on the swing and let out a huge sigh of relief. "Wow am I glad that's over! I never want to do anything like that ever again!"

"Great job!" enthused Lance. "Passports – that's incredible! What did the men talk about?" Lance and Joel listened eagerly as Ravi and Debbie recounted the rest of their adventure and grimaced as they heard of the new man's threat to the driver.

"Something criminal is going on, for sure," said Lance soberly when they had finished their tale. "You don't get passports just like that."

"How many do you think there were, Debs?" asked Joel.

Debbie shrugged. "I'm not sure. Twenty, maybe thirty? I didn't get a proper look, but I saw the cover of the one at the top, that's how I know they were passports."

"And what about the lorry?" Ravi asked Joel and Lance. "It's empty then?"

"Seems to be," replied Lance. "Nobody answered when we knocked. We wrote its registration number in our phones and the other man's too – in fact we took everyone's who came in the car park; we've just deleted the ones we don't need any more."

"You wrote them in messages!" said Debbie. "That was clever!"

"You can't see it from here, but the boss man's got a really smart silver Audi, brand new!" added Joel.

"Good work," nodded Ravi.

"OK then, so let's put all our information together," said Lance in a business-like manner. "So far, we know that people are being taken in the lorry to the Tills Tiles warehouse, people who seem to want to get out. Some at least are staying there at night, because we heard a baby there. The driver of the lorry appears to be working for the man who came in the Audi. Anything else to add?" He looked round at his friends.

"Well," said Joel, "on the first night the people in the lorry seemed to want us to know they were there, but when we called up last night there was no reply. That could mean they've been threatened to keep quiet."

"That's possible," nodded Lance.

Debbie nodded too. "Now we know what sort of evil people we're dealing with, that would make sense. Also," she continued, "the passports mean that the people are probably foreign."

"Were they British passports, Debs?" asked Ravi.

"I think so. They were red on the outside . . . but I don't know what any others would look like," she admitted.

"If the passports were for the people in the lorry, that doesn't make sense," said Joel. "They don't need British passports if they're already in Britain!"

"And what are those men doing with people in their lorry anyway?" wondered Ravi. "Surely they're not slaves? Not in this country?" Debbie shook her head.

"No, there aren't slaves any more," she said. "The slave trade was abolished hundreds of years ago. We saw a video of it in history."

"What about in other countries though?" asked Ravi.

"But that doesn't make sense either," objected Debbie. "Why would people be smuggled into this country, then given passports to go and be slaves somewhere else? Anyway, are there slaves anywhere else?" Everyone racked their brains, but nobody could come up with a solution to that problem.

"We need more information," admitted Lance eventually.

"Maybe we should just go to the police now," said Debbie. "If one man is giving another man lots of passports, that's definitely not right, everyone has to apply for their own. I think the police would take it seriously."

"But suppose the police get the passports but not the people in the warehouse?" asked Ravi. "To God, the people are the most important thing."

"That's true," nodded Lance.

"Pity we can't follow the lorry," remarked Joel. "It would be useful to know where it goes when it's not at the warehouse. But we could carry on with the research plan. Like Lance says, we need more info."

"First, how about you and me running down to the tile shop quickly?" Ravi suggested to Lance.

"What for?" asked Debbie. "The shop will be open."

"Exactly!" said Ravi. "We can go in! There might be a clue in the shop, we might even find out where the people are hiding . . . or being hidden. And if we do find people locked up, then we can go to the police straight away!"

"But suppose the driver comes with the lorry while we're there?" asked Lance uneasily.

"He probably only goes there after the shop's closed," shrugged Ravi.

"So we'd be safe," nodded Lance. "Could do then. Do you two agree?" He looked at Joel and Debbie, who were both looking a bit glum. "I wish you could come too!"

"Oh well," sighed Joel. "Life is tough!"

"Somebody's got to look after Willow, anyway," said Debbie generously. "We can walk with you the first bit of the way, then wait for you to come back."

"Better wait here and watch for the lorry leaving," said

Ravi. "If it comes in our direction, let us know and we'll get out quick!"

"As the lorry's empty at the moment," said Joel, "you should be OK. If the man was going to drop people off, they're already there, or if he's got to go and pick them up from somewhere else first, he'll be ages."

"Very clever, Joel!" admired Debbie.

"I am indeed, dear Sister!" grinned Joel. "I'm glad you see it at last!"

"OK then Ravi," said Lance. "Let's go now!"

"So we'll stay here and watch," said Debbie. "How long do you think you'll be?"

"Half an hour, max," said Ravi, looking at his watch. "It's 11 o'clock now. We should easily be back by half past."

"Keep texting us then," said Debbie. "Then we won't worry."

"And we'll text you if the lorry leaves," added Joel.

"OK," agreed Lance. "See you later then!"

*　*　*

On their own in the park, the first ten minutes passed slowly for Joel and Debbie. First they played a chasing game with Willow, well away from the café but in sight of the car park, so they would notice if the driver appeared. After that, Debbie suggested they have a closer look at the lorry. "Might as well," shrugged Joel. "There's nothing much else to do. We'll have to keep a watch out for the driver though. Willow's got to stay hidden too, remember?"

"Of course," agreed Debbie. "But you never know, we might find out something useful." At the edge of the car park they paused and looked round. Apart from an elderly couple loading shopping into an old Fiat it was quite empty, so they ran quickly to the lorry. Joel jumped when his mobile bleeped. It was only a text from Lance, which said, "In tile shp. Nthng yet." Joel replied, "All still here. Bored. :-("

"Twenty more minutes," sighed Joel. While Debbie searched all round the lorry for clues, Joel drew a large smiley face with spiky hair in the dirt on the back of the lorry and wrote, "This version also in white". He grinned at his handiwork and called Debbie to come and have a look.

"Oh how childish!" she scoffed when she saw it. "I've actually been doing something useful."

"Oh really, Clever Debber!" said Joel. "Well I think there's a bit of an artist in me and I needed to express my talent!"

"You do talk rubbish sometimes, Joel," said Debbie loftily. "While you've been playing, I've found out some useful information!"

"Oh yeah?"

"Actually, yes. It was difficult to see much – the cab's really high up, but there's an empty sandwich packet in the cab, on the shelf by the windscreen. The writing on it's in French."

"So he's been abroad with the lorry!" said Joel, listening more intently. "Perhaps he is bringing back illegal immigrants then!"

"Makes it look more likely, doesn't it?"

"Not bad, Debs!" said Joel. "Could be useful info. We'll tell the others when they get back."

"Shall I go and see what the driver's doing now?" asked Debbie. "He's taking a long time over his breakfast!"

"You can if you want," replied Joel. "I'm not going anywhere near him. If you do, I'll go and play with Willow again."

"Don't go far then," said Debbie, but he didn't get the chance. As he reached the edge of the car park, Debbie ran back up to him, breathless and pale.

"Quick, hide!" she panted. "The driver's coming this way, with another man!"

NINE

Back to the Warehouse

Debbie and Joel both shot behind some bushes at the edge of the car park, crept along to where they could see the lorry and crouched down, waiting anxiously for the men to come in to view. While they were waiting, Joel's mobile bleeped again. "Is everything OK?" asked Debbie.

"Just Rav letting us know they're going to sneak into the warehouse," replied Joel. "Rather them than me! Don't bark, Willow," he warned the little dog, as the men came closer. She wagged her tail and shoved her nose in his face, almost knocking him off balance. She loved being in the park with friends! "Willow, you have no idea," said Joel fondly, stroking her silky ears.

"They're coming!" hissed Debbie.

Suddenly recognising the second man, Joel took in a sharp breath. "What?" asked Debbie anxiously.

"The other man's the one who opened the warehouse doors on the night of the treasure hunt," said Joel. "He's wearing the same filthy boiler suit."

"They must have been talking in the café!" gasped Debbie, looking shocked. "A second meeting! We should have been listening to that!"

Joel nodded. "We didn't think, did we? I wonder if

they're going to drive the lorry to the tile shop now?"

"Better text the others! No, phone, that way we'll know they've got the message."

"Just hang on a minute, see which way the lorry goes," suggested Joel, peering round the bushes.

"No, now! It'll give them an extra few minutes to get away!" Debbie tried Ravi's number, then Lance's, but there was a problem. "They've both got their phones turned off!" she said, surprised and not a little worried. "I wonder why?"

She tried again; Joel tried too, to no avail, then looked up with a sinking feeling as the lorry swung out of the car park towards the industrial estate. "Why would they turn their phones off?" wailed Debbie.

Joel swallowed hard. "Maybe they've got no signal where they are?"

"They did a minute ago!"

"We'll have to follow the lorry then," said Joel urgently, scrabbling quickly to his feet. "If those men catch Ravi and Lance in the warehouse they'll be for it! Quick, Debs, we've got to go and warn them!"

"We'll never get there in time," wailed Debbie as they left the park at a run. "And anyway we're not allowed! I don't want to be in this any more, it's too horrible. Let's go home and get Mum and Dad!"

"There's no time!" argued Joel, picking up speed. "Come on, Lance and Ravi are in the warehouse now!"

"Don't wait for me and Willow, then, we're not as fast as you!" urged Debbie. So leaving Willow and Debbie behind, Joel ran as fast as he could to the edge of the industrial estate. He was a good runner, but by the time he could see Tills Tiles, his breath was coming in gasps and his legs felt like jelly. He stopped and stared, hoping desperately that the lorry wouldn't be there. Perhaps it had been going somewhere else after all? But there it stood, on the forecourt, waiting to enter the warehouse; even from that distance he could see his silly smiley face and daft message. Ravi and Lance were nowhere to be seen. While Joel stood there, his thoughts coming in jumbled heaps, the lorry drove slowly into the warehouse, like an animal closing in on its prey. By the time Debbie and Willow joined Joel, the doors had closed behind it.

"Is the lorry there? Have you seen Ravi and Lance?" Debbie panted.

Joel grimaced and tried to make his voice sound normal, although he felt like yelling aloud. "The lorry's just gone in the warehouse."

"Are you sure?"

"Saw it with my own eyes. I haven't seen Lance and Ravi. I suppose they must still be in there."

Tears sprang to Debbie's eyes. "Oh no!" she wailed. "Everything's going wrong! And we didn't even pray!"

* * *

It hadn't taken Ravi and Lance long to get to Tills Tiles. The daytime transformation of the industrial estate amazed them. It was so busy! Nobody looked at the two lads; everyone was getting on with their own affairs. Cars, vans and lorries were zipping by on the road and the boys had to watch for traffic pulling in and out of parking spaces on the forecourts that had been deserted on the last two evenings. No echo there now; it was sometimes difficult to be heard over the general noise of traffic and machinery. Lance nearly got run over by a forklift truck coming out of one of the warehouses; Ravi grabbed him just in time.

"Blend in, look round, pretend to be with this couple," said Ravi quietly, as they followed a grey-haired couple into the tile shop. Once in, Lance sent a quick message to Joel and received one back.

"They're bored!" grinned Lance and Ravi laughed.

"Pity they couldn't come too, but it's probably just as well. Four of us might have attracted too much attention, especially with Willow." The shop was just as Lance remembered it from the night before, but come to life. It was light and airy, a bit chilly and smelled somehow of new houses and the technology workshop at school. Pop music from the seventies added atmosphere. There were three members of staff; a teenage girl serving on the till, a middle-aged woman advising a young couple and a bald man stacking up boxes of tiles on a display near the front door. They were easy to pick out because they were wearing red and yellow Tills Tiles sweatshirts. There were quite a few customers looking round the shop, mostly couples. One lady was holding up lengths of fabric next to various tile displays. Two small children, who seemed to think that the tile shop was a playground, were running round chasing each other, shrieking with laughter.

Lance and Ravi followed the older couple at a safe distance, looking round for anything unusual. At the back of the shop a door labelled "STAFF ONLY" was propped open with a blue plastic chair. Through the door they could see what appeared to be a staff room, furnished with a scattering of tatty red chairs, a small fridge and a cupboard with a kettle and assorted crockery on top. The fire exit they had seen the previous night was there too. "Nothing interesting there," observed Ravi.

"No, they wouldn't prop the door open if there was anything dodgy going on," agreed Lance. "Let's see if we can't get a look in the warehouse bit." Fortunately, the couple they were following stopped to consider a display of floor tiles not far from the door to the warehouse and spoke to the man stacking tiles.

"If we haven't got them in stock," said the man, "we should be able to get them in a couple of weeks. I'll have a look for you."

"He's going in the warehouse!" whispered Ravi, as the man walked purposefully towards the door.

"Perfect!" nodded Lance. "If we get a chance, we'll go and have a quick look round, OK?"

"Might as well," agreed Ravi. "I'll text Joel, tell him what we're doing." The man returned, carrying a couple of tiles in his hand.

"These are the closest we've got," he said to the couple. Ravi and Lance grinned at each other. He had left the door open! They edged closer, then when nobody was looking, they slipped in.

TEN
A Secret Door

The warehouse was huge, damp and cold with a characterless feel about it. There were no windows; bright lights hanging from the ceiling lit up circles below them, but cast hard shadows into the gloom. The part of the warehouse nearest the road was completely empty. "That's where the lorry comes in," Lance whispered to Ravi, who nodded. The rest of the warehouse was full of shelves with row upon row of boxes. There were also piles of boxes stacked on the floor.

"These are all tiles!" breathed Ravi. "Can you believe that?" Just as he spoke, they heard the man returning to the warehouse. Both boys scrambled quickly behind a stack of boxes. The shop man put the tiles he was carrying into an open box then went straight back into the shop, turning the lights off with a loud click and closing the door behind him. Lance and Ravi suddenly found themselves in pitch darkness. "Oops!" said Ravi. Lance could tell he was grinning from the way he spoke. He grinned back, although Ravi couldn't see.

"Did you notice where the light switch was?" he asked.

"It's got to be near the door," said Ravi, then laughed aloud. "Now this is what you call a real adventure!" The

boys took a few fumbling steps in the dark round their
stack of boxes, but Lance stumbled into the edge of a
metal shelf.

"Ouch," he groaned, rubbing his shin. "That really
hurt!"

"Better wait here a minute for our eyes to get used to
the dark," suggested Ravi. "Perhaps the man will be back
soon; we'll need to get out quick while we can."

"What are we going to say if he sees us?"

"I don't know, we'd better think of something quick. He
looked a decent sort of man though, didn't he, not like a
crook or anything. Probably doesn't know about the lorry."

"You can't tell by appearances," said Lance with
feeling. "Me and Joel had a friend once called Frankie,
whose dad seemed really nice, but he was fiddling money
at his work. Loads of money, thousands. In the end he
went to prison for it, ask Joel, he'll tell you. You know in
the Bible it says that man judges by outward appearances,
but God looks at the heart? That is so true. We felt sorry
for Frankie. He didn't know anything about what his dad
was doing and he had to move away."

"That's awful," said Ravi. "So you think the shop man
might be in this too?"

"You just can't tell – maybe they all are."

"Not the girl on the till? She doesn't look much older
than us! Well, you know the man who met the driver in
the café? You'd never have taken him for a criminal, would
you, if you just saw him in the street?"

"Exactly!" agreed Lance. "And the lorry driver called you a Paki, but I bet you don't even know where Pakistan is!"

"Well, not really!" admitted Ravi and they both laughed.

Just then Lance let out an exclamation. "We are so stupid! Our mobiles have got lights! And shall we text Joel and Debbie again? – Oh, I've got no signal in here, have you?" Ravi tried his phone, then shook his head.

"No, shame, this would have made them laugh!" The glow from the two mobile phones didn't exactly light up the whole warehouse, but it was enough to make a difference and the boys edged towards the door. Suddenly Lance stopped. "Shouldn't we be looking round and listening for clues, not trying to escape?" he remembered.

"Oh yes!" agreed Ravi. "Your leg OK?"

"I'll probably get a bruise – it's all right though," replied Lance. They turned back, but a noise stopped them in their tracks. It was the sound they least wanted to hear. A lorry had driven up to the warehouse doors and was waiting outside, engine still running. "Hide, quick!" said Lance, stumbling in the darkness back to the stack of boxes, his heart suddenly beating faster.

"It must be a different lorry, bringing tiles or something," said Ravi, "or Joel would have . . ." and they both realised at the same time. Joel couldn't text them. They had no signal. "This could really be oops this time," swallowed Ravi. Lance nodded slowly. Peering anxiously round the boxes, he watched the huge doors slide open.

Daylight flooded in and through the glare of the cheerful sunshine, the outline of a dirty white lorry could clearly be seen.

"Oh no!" breathed Lance, a sinking feeling hitting his stomach. "It's our lorry." And the man who was opening the doors was none other than the small, mean-looking man who had jumped out of the cab on the night of the treasure hunt.

The noise as the lorry drove inside the warehouse was ear-splitting. With nowhere else for the sound to go, the powerful engine's roar echoed round and round the building, filling it with the most horrendous cacophony of sound. The boys' relief as the engine cut out was tempered by the loss of daylight again as the warehouse doors clanged shut behind the lorry.

"Pity they didn't leave the doors open," whispered Ravi, his voice sounding a little shaky. Lance nodded, but couldn't reply. He held his breath and melted further into the shadows as the driver switched the lorry's headlights on and the smaller man's footsteps approached the shop door. He opened it and called out, "We'll just be in here a minute, Dave, OK?" Ravi breathed in sharply.

"You were right," he whispered as the man bolted the door top and bottom. Lance grimaced. At least the man hadn't switched the warehouse lights on. He wondered if they could make it to the shop unseen, hugging the walls? In his head he measured the distance; it couldn't be more than six metres, but they would have to run; there was nothing to hide them once they left the shelter of the boxes. He whispered his idea to Ravi, who shook his head.

"Too dangerous. Let's just wait — they don't know we're here. If someone comes this way though . . ."

From where he crouched, Lance could see the driver in the cab. At first he was looking at some paperwork on a clipboard, then suddenly he jumped down. Lance tensed, ready to run if he needed to, but the driver walked straight to the back of the building, unaware that he was being watched. By the light of the lorry's headlights he moved a box from a shelf to reveal a handle and opened a small door, which was completely concealed by a metal shelf unit. "A secret door!" gasped Lance. "Look, Ravi, the door opens with the shelves still on it!"

ELEVEN

The Captives

"What are we going to do now?" Joel asked Debbie worriedly, staring at the empty forecourt where the lorry had been standing.

"I'm going to phone Mum," said Debbie, quickly wiping away a tear before it fell. "She'll know what to do!" But just as her mum answered her phone the line went dead. "Oh no, my battery's gone," groaned Debbie, her voice shaking. "You'll have to phone, Joel!"

"I'll probably run out of credit if Mum wants to know everything. Which she will," replied Joel slowly. "I could text though?" There was a minute's silence, broken by a family walking by. Debbie looked down and pretended to be using her phone; she didn't want people to see she had been crying.

"OK," she replied eventually.

"What shall I say?"

"Ask her if we can go in the tile shop while it's open."

Joel grimaced. "She'd better not say no!"

Debbie swallowed hard. "I think we should ask," she said. "Nobody can do anything to us in the shop." She thought of the café earlier on, and Ravi's cheerful assurance. Some other words came back to her too, which

Lance had said, "If it's God's will, then he'll protect us." And suddenly she knew that He would. "And ask Mum to pray," she added, as Joel began to type the message. "Dad too, if he's there."

It seemed forever that they waited in silence for a reply, staring at the warehouse, hoping that Ravi and Lance would suddenly appear, laughing and joking and the text message wouldn't matter. But while they waited, with no sign of their friends, the lorry slowly emerged from the warehouse, like an animal emerging from its lair. It paused while the small man closed the doors behind it.

Joel's mobile bleeped. "Well?" asked Debbie, feeling like screaming. "What does she say?"

"She says 'OK, only while shop's open; remember back for lunch,'" read Joel hurriedly. "'Will pray.'"

"OK let's go then!" said Debbie, starting to run.

"But we've got to stop the lorry!" panicked Joel as it picked up speed. He started to run along the road towards the lorry, waving his arms and shouting.

"Don't ignore me!" shouted Joel as it sped away. "Where are my friends?" But the lorry just kept on going. Debbie stayed rooted to the spot. "It didn't stop," yelled Joel, running back to Debbie. "Suppose Lance and Ravi are in there?"

*   *   *

"We'd never have found that!" agreed Ravi, peering over Lance's shoulder to see the hidden door.

"A secret room!" whispered Lance. "Maybe the people are in there. Better check what the other man's doing," he added. They peered cautiously round the other side of the boxes, saw nothing, but jumped in alarm as they heard the back of the lorry rattle and clang open. For a minute there was a dreadful silence. Lance thought that Ravi must be able to hear his heart beating, it was thumping so loudly in his chest. "You watch for him, I'll watch the driver," Lance suggested, turning his attention back to the secret door. What he saw almost took his breath away. The driver was standing there, arms folded, while one by one people were appearing from the hidden room. They were of all ages and skin colours; old, young, men, women and even children. Some carried bundles, one woman carried a baby. They walked silently towards the lorry in single file. They looked exhausted, thin and gaunt, frightened and hopeless. Some looked round desperately, others hardly looked round at all. Their clothes were dirty, their appearance was one of neglect.

"The baby!" breathed Lance, more to himself than to Ravi, who was also watching in stunned silence as the row of people moved towards the back of the lorry.

"Single file!" growled the driver menacingly as a young woman caught up with an old man in front of her. Turning round to see what was happening, the old man stumbled, but was hauled harshly to his feet. "Get up, Grandad," growled the driver. A younger man resisted, realising they had to get in the lorry. He began to speak emphatically in a foreign language. "Silence!" hissed the driver, but the man kept talking, faster and louder, making gestures with his arms. He looked desperate, like a hunted animal still hoping for mercy but knowing it would get none. As his voice became more frenzied, the driver grabbed a terrified girl by her arm. She couldn't have been more than five years old. He hissed harshly to the man, "Shut up and get in or I hurt the girl, see?" Lance watched in horror as the man squeezed the little girl's arm. He wanted to shout, but no sound would come out. The girl looked terrified. She bit her lip and gave a frightened whimper. A tear dripped down her dirty face. The bold man shut up and with a look of tired defeat, walked in his turn to the back of the lorry. Lance could feel tears welling up in his own eyes. These were real people! "Oh God," he cried out silently, "don't let them do this!"

"Everybody in, Wayne?" called the driver from the back of the lorry, when all the people had disappeared from view.

"Yup, that's it!" replied Wayne cheerfully, unbolting the door to the shop. His cheerfulness was sickening. He might have been loading sacks of potatoes. Lance made a face at Ravi, who also had tears in his eyes.

"Is this real?" muttered Ravi. Lance grimaced and shifted position. As he did so, he felt his foot knock against something. It was a large broom and as soon as he saw it, Lance knew it was going to fall. He drew an involuntary breath and made a grab for the handle, but it was too late. In what seemed like slow motion, the broom slid down the wall behind him. Lance and Ravi stared at each other in horror as it came to rest with a harsh clatter on the floor.

"Aha, someone thought they could get away, did they?" said Wayne. "That's a mistake!" There was no time to think. As the man approached from the front, the boys scooted to the back. Looking wildly round, it seemed there was nowhere else to go but through the little door which led to the secret room. The harsh glare of the lorry's headlights hit the back wall, but the driver was nowhere to be seen and the lights were not all-seeing, they didn't reach the corners of the room. Ravi shot to the left and squeezed behind an old sofa; Lance ran to the right and curled up under a little table, melting himself into the wall as best he could. The room stank and Lance was fast becoming more frightened than he had ever been in his life before. Unanswerable questions came to him thick and fast. Had Wayne or the driver spotted them? Would they be discovered? What if they got shut in?

TWELVE

Imprisoned!

Lance held his breath to keep out the stench of the secret room, which was making him feel sick. In the distance, he heard Wayne call out, "False alarm, broom falling over!" Lance sighed with relief.

"Hurry up then," called the driver. "Let's get shot of this lot, I'm sick of their filth. I'll check the room, make sure." Lance took another deep breath. He squeezed his eyes tightly closed as he heard the driver's footsteps come towards their hiding place, step by step. He doesn't know we're here, thought Lance, his heart pounding fit to bust. And if he doesn't find us, he'll shut us in. Is that better than being caught? There was a pause; evidently the driver was looking into the room. Lance desperately tried to think straight. Maybe they should give themselves up? Then the decision was taken away from him; the door was closed and once more he and Ravi were plunged into darkness, a thick, heavy, cloying blackness that could almost be felt. Lance heard the box being slid back on the shelf to hide the handle and a minute later the muffled sound of the lorry's engine roar to life once more.

"You there, Rav?" asked Lance from under his table, as the engine began to fade away.

"Right here somewhere!" came back Ravi's muted voice as he eased himself out backwards from behind the settee. "They didn't see us!"

"Is that good or bad?" wondered Lance aloud, crawling out from under the table.

"Actually, bad, probably, thinking about it," said Ravi, feeling for the door and discovering that it didn't have a handle on their side. "And doesn't this place smell awful!" His voice sounded wobbly, like he was trying to be brave but didn't feel it. He put his shoulder to the door, but it didn't budge. Outside, the garage doors closed with a clang. It sounded like hope fading.

"Perhaps we shouldn't have run in here," admitted Lance. "We should have run to the shop instead."

"Impossible, we'd have had to pass that Wayne man."

"Well, Joel and Debbie know we're here," Lance reminded him.

"They know we came in the warehouse, but they don't know we're imprisoned here."

"They'll tell their parents though, when we don't go back, then someone will come and look for us?" There was a short, uncomfortable silence. "Then we're going to get in trouble!"

"I don't care about trouble, I just want to get out of here!" said Ravi. "If we hear anybody out there, we'll have to shout really loudly. Do you think Dave from the shop knows about this room? It's really well hidden, isn't it?"

"I bet he does know. But they won't want anyone else

to know, will they? He might not tell our parents, or the police or whatever, that we're here. Even if people come looking for us, they might not find us."

"That's a scary thought," admitted Ravi.

"Let's change the subject," suggested Lance. "I wonder if there's anything to eat or drink in here?"

"Might be. No, there probably isn't any food," Ravi corrected himself. "Did you see the state of those poor people?"

"Yes, I could hardly believe what I was seeing. I wonder how long they were here, this room's really small, they must have been well squashed up. No wonder it stinks."

"It's like a thin strip, isn't it, running across the warehouse. Quite clever really, the way they've done it."

"In a grim sort of way, I suppose," nodded Lance.

"Some of them were probably in the lorry the night of the treasure hunt," said Ravi. "They looked like they were from lots of different countries, don't you think? And wasn't it awful when that man started talking and the driver squeezed that girl's arm?"

"I could hardly believe what I was seeing," nodded Lance. "But," he added, "perhaps us being in here is all part of God's plan."

"How do you mean?" asked Ravi rather dubiously.

"I don't know exactly," admitted Lance. "But remember in Sunday Club a few weeks ago, we did about Peter in prison? It was like everything had gone wrong, but an angel came and let him out!"

"So we need an angel!" agreed Ravi with a grin, then laughed aloud, making Lance jump. "Maybe Joel will be our angel!" Lance laughed too and suddenly felt more cheerful.

"Nothing's impossible for the Lord, we know that. Somehow we'll get out, God is in control. And is it me, or are your eyes getting used to the dark as well?"

"No, it's not just you, mine are too," said Ravi. Then he gasped, "Look, up there, those are the two windows we saw last night, covered up with something!"

"You're right!" remembered Lance. "We'll have to yell if we hear someone out there."

"Remember when we called up last night? Those people must have been able to hear us. Joel was right, they must have been told not to reply."

"I wonder where they're being taken now?" There was a short silence. Lance thought of the girl whose arm the driver had grabbed. "I think we ought to pray," he said soberly. "We should have done that a long time ago."

"You're right," admitted Ravi. "If we ever needed an answer to prayer, it's now."

*   *   *

"Why didn't the lorry stop?" yelled Joel. "What are we going to do now?"

"Maybe Lance and Ravi are still in the shop!" said Debbie. "Suppose they're tied up or something? Or they might just be hiding and come out in a minute, maybe the men didn't see them. We've got to go and find out."

"OK," agreed Joel, swallowing hard. His heart was beating faster. Every moment he was hoping to see Lance and Ravi smiling cheerfully and running towards them, but somehow, uninvited, the thought of his friends bound and gagged came to mind and a sick, heavy feeling grew in the pit of his stomach.

"Are dogs allowed in shops?" Debbie asked as they approached Tills Tiles at a run. Joel shrugged. "I'll just walk in," Debbie muttered, more to herself than to her brother. "Willow's small, by the time anybody's noticed, we'll hopefully be back out again."

Joel reached the door first; he looked through it, then seeing nothing untoward, pushed the door open and walked in. Nobody seemed to notice them, even with Willow. Everything looked disconcertingly normal, but there was no sign of Ravi or Lance. "Oh God, where are they?" thought Joel desperately. The door to the warehouse was closed, he noticed with a grimace.

"Shall we look round the shop first?" Debbie asked, trying to make her voice sound normal. Joel nodded, but a quick tour of the shop revealed nothing.

They stopped right next to the door to the warehouse. Debbie pretended to look at some tiles on the wall.

"I suppose we'll just have to open the door and go in," she said, with her back to the shop. "You turn round, see if anyone's watching. I don't want to attract attention with Willow."

"Are we both going in?" asked Joel.

"Do you want to go in on your own?" Debbie asked him rather icily, picking up the little dog.

"Would you rather stay here?"

"No, I think we should stay together," swallowed Debbie. "Hurry up! Is anybody looking?" Joel turned round. Some people were walking past to leave the shop.

"Don't go yet," he cautioned. "When I say, you go in with Willow, I'll follow." Debbie nodded.

"OK," she agreed. "You shut the door then." Suddenly the coast was clear.

"Now!" hissed Joel and they shot into the warehouse. "Wow, it's dark in here," he muttered, pulling the door quietly closed. "Where are the lights?"

"Is there anybody there?" whispered Debbie into the still darkness. Silence. She tried again, a little louder. Still no reply. Willow whimpered. "Now what?" asked Debbie anxiously. Now that nobody could see, she allowed the tears that she had been holding back to drip down her face. "It doesn't look like they're here, does it? Maybe we ought to go back."

THIRTEEN
Praises in Prison

"And there was light!" said Joel, finding the light switches by the door with his fingers. He was trying to sound cheerful, but it didn't really work. There were three switches in a row; he pressed just one, which lit up the other side of the warehouse. It was still a bit dingy where they were standing, but at least they could see.

Debbie wiped her face quickly.

"Lance, Ravi?" she called, looking round as she stepped out. Nobody answered, but her voice echoed round. This was too much for Willow, who barked, once, loudly.

"Shhhh Willow!" hissed Joel, looking worriedly at the door. Nobody came.

"This is awful!" wailed Debbie. "And with the lights on, if anyone comes in they'll know someone's here!"

"Stop moaning!" muttered Joel. "Let's just run quickly round."

"Suppose they've got them in the lorry?" panicked Debbie, echoing Joel's thoughts.

"Don't think about it," advised Joel. "Follow me!" They zig-zagged around the rows of shelves, calling quietly as they searched, keeping an ear-out for the sound of the

shop door opening. Then, as they approached the back of
the warehouse, Willow took a sudden leap forward and
started to sniff the floor. She ran to a stack of boxes,
Debbie in tow, then ran and sniffed the back wall, her tail
wagging.

"They were here!" cried Debbie.

"We know that, they texted us," said Joel testily.

"Don't be like that!" Debbie replied, feeling encouraged.
"Find them, Willow, where's Ravi?"

"Let's go back," groaned Joel. "This is hopeless. Maybe
Lance and Ravi were hiding here, but they're not here now,
that's obvious, we've searched the whole place. We'd better
go and tell Mum and Dad before the lorry gets any further.
We ought to go back anyway, it's nearly lunch time."
Debbie paused uncertainly, then started to cry again.

"Not in the lorry," she said, shaking her head. "They
can't be in the lorry!" She took a step towards the door
but Willow nearly yanked the lead out of her hand.
"Willow thinks they're still here," said Debbie, puzzled,
staring at the back wall covered with shelves.

"Shut up Debs!" yelled Joel suddenly. "Listen!" Debbie
listened. She could hear traffic on the road outside, the
beat of pop music from the shop, the sound of a car door
closing. But rather thin and faraway she could also clearly
hear the sound of singing. She recognised the song.

With Jesus we have victory
If we trust in him,

We don't need horse or chariots
If we've confessed our sin!
We have to stand and fight,
The word of God's our sword,
Our enemies will run away,
'Cause Jesus is our Lord!

"They're singing!" Joel almost yelled in his excitement. "It's Ravi and Lance! Well done, Willow, you've found them!"

"But where are they?" asked Debbie. She looked around in bewilderment. Willow barked and scraped the wall with her paws by a wire rack of shelving. The singing abruptly stopped and a muffled voice came through the wall.

"Is that you Willow, Joel, Debbie? Get us out of here!" yelled Lance at the top of his voice.

"Don't shout, someone will hear us!" urged Joel, looking in vain for a door.

"We're so glad you're alive," called Debbie. "We thought you might have been taken away in the lorry!"

"Hurry up and get us out!" shouted Ravi. "We sort of got shut in by mistake!"

"But how do you get in?" asked Joel. With Lance calling out instructions and Debbie soothing a very excited little dog, Joel soon had the door open and Lance and Ravi burst out, rubbing and blinking their eyes in the light, dim though it was. After a joyful reunion and a few tears, not only from Debbie, there was a moment's silence.

"Thanks for letting us out!" said Ravi gratefully.

"There were people here," said Lance.

"We saw the lorry go in and come out again!" said Joel. "We wondered if you'd been taken away!"

"They loaded up the lorry with the people who were in this room," said Lance.

"It was awful," added Ravi solemnly. "But let's get out of here, then we'll tell you all about it."

"Shall we go through the shop?" asked Joel. As he spoke, another lorry could be heard drawing up to the warehouse doors. There was a moment's frightened silence.

"Where's the best place to hide?" asked Debbie, fear in her eyes.

"No more hiding!" groaned Ravi, hugging his little dog.

"I agree!" said Lance. "Let's get right by the doors, then as soon as they open, we'll all rush out together past the lorry or whatever it is and run for home, OK?"

"Excellent idea," agreed Joel, his eyes shining, though his heart was thumping hard in his chest. "Take them by surprise."

"What if it's the lorry coming back?" asked Debbie anxiously.

"I don't care what lorry it is or who's in it," said Ravi firmly, making for the doors as they began to slide open. "I'm going home!"

FOURTEEN
Real Treasure

"Can you believe it's only a week since we were here in Ravi's bedroom eating our last treasure prize?" Joel asked the others, stretching out on a rug on the floor and rifling through a second box of chocolates for his favourite caramel toffee. Ravi and Lance laughed, but Debbie snatched the box from his hands.

"Excuse me," she retorted, "you lost the last treasure hunt! Remember? It was my prize, mine and Ravi's!"

"Whatever!" muttered Joel lazily, unwrapping his toffee. "We all won this one, anyway! We should keep this up, we'll never have to buy our own sweets again!"

"It was really kind of Tina to buy us another treasure prize," said Ravi, grinning. "But I'm not sure I want to do anything like that again!"

"I certainly never want to see another dirty white lorry again as long as I live," admitted Joel. He shuddered and paused dramatically. "And from now on, I'm going to express my artistic talents . . . anywhere but on dirty lorries! You know, I'm so glad the second lorry, the one delivering tiles, was red, not white. I think I might have gone mad!" The others all laughed.

"We well shocked the delivery man, didn't we, bursting

out of the warehouse like that!" grinned Lance. "He stared like he couldn't believe his eyes! I thought he was going to drop his precious tiles!"

"It was your singing that got me," said Debbie. "I thought for a minute you'd died and gone to heaven and were singing with the angels!" The others burst out laughing.

"I can't believe you were singing!" said Joel.

"Well, remember in the Bible it says about Paul and someone singing in jail?" asked Lance.

"It was Paul and Silas, Dad looked it up," Ravi informed him.

"Whoever, well, we thought we'd do the same, didn't we Rav? It was dead dark in there, it absolutely stank and it was well scary. We had to do something. We tried *Power of God* first, but it didn't work without instruments, there's too many gaps."

"So we decided on *With Jesus we have Victory*," cut in Ravi. "It sounded a bit strange at first, with just the two of us, but we soon got in to it. I tell you what, I really meant it too! I was even doing the actions – it was great – not that anyone could see!" Everyone laughed again.

"How could it have been great, being locked up in that horrible smelly room?" asked Debbie incredulously.

"God was with us," said Ravi simply and Lance agreed.

"We were sort of worried to start with, but then we remembered that nothing is impossible with the Lord and we knew he'd do something. We even laughed about Joel being an angel sent to open the door. When he did, well that was just so amazing!" They all fell about laughing as Joel did an impression of an angel with wings, fluttering down from the sky.

"Admit it, I saved your lives," said Joel, grinning. "Anyone want to kiss my feet?"

"Oh thank you," breathed Lance pretending to gratefully kiss his feet.

"Oh disgusting, you two!" groaned Debbie.

"Actually I think we can safely say that it was the Lord who saved us all," said Ravi. "We could all easily have been captured and . . . well, goodness knows what could have happened . . ."

"The best thing is," said Lance solemnly, "those horrible men have been stopped from doing those awful things to those people."

"Can you believe they brought them over here from wherever they could, tricking them into thinking they were coming to a better life, then making them work for them!" said Debbie, shaking her head.

"And the people thought they were getting real passports, but they were fakes," added Joel. "What a scam!"

"I'm so glad the police caught lots of the gang," said Debbie. "That was so useful that I saw that French sandwich packet, that's why they checked the ports."

"You're never going to let us forget that, are you?" sighed Joel ruefully, "even though it was because of my work of art they caught the lorry so quickly on the motorway!"

"Oh shut up you two," said Lance. "If you're going to

argue, wait 'til you get home!"

"So, who's for more treasure?" asked Ravi, handing round the chocolate box. "I think we all did well. I mean, you know there's bad things going on, you hear it in the news, but actually seeing it with your own eyes and doing something about it . . ." he shook his head and struggled for words. "I don't think it's sunk in properly yet." The others nodded agreement.

"I hope that nice police woman doesn't forget to let us know what happens to those people," said Debbie.

Lance nodded. "I shall never forget the way they looked as long as I live. I'm so glad we did our bit to help them. The police were onto the gang, but that particular lorry load of people might not have been saved."

"Scary, but definitely worth it," agreed Joel. "Willow, stop staring at me like that, I'm not going to give you any chocolate!"

"I've suddenly thought of something," said Debbie. "Remember what Tina said at youth club about every person being treasured by God?"

"No," answered Lance and Joel in unison.

"You must do," Debbie assured them. "Three points to treasure, remember that? It was the idea behind her organising the treasure hunt, to show us that seeking God is seeking treasure, and sharing the gospel with people is sharing treasure and every person is treasured by God!"

"I don't remember any of that," said Joel, shaking his head.

"That's 'cause you missed the talk!" laughed Ravi. "You and Lance were still out looking for 007 on the industrial estate!"

"Oh yes!" remembered Lance and they all laughed.

"Well what I was going to say," continued Debbie, "is that those people in the lorry are the real treasure, not these chocolates."

"You don't have to have them if you don't want them, Debs!" said Ravi quickly. "We can have your share! No, seriously, I know what you mean."

"You should have seen them," said Lance. "Not the chocolates! The people, I mean. They were all thin and hopeless-looking. We ought to keep praying for them. Maybe some of them are Christians already. And one day I think I'm going to go abroad somewhere foreign to help poor people and show them how much Jesus loves them."

"I bet you will," said Debbie. "I might too."

"Maybe we all will!" said Ravi, "But we don't have to wait 'til we're older to do stuff, we've found that out."

"That's true!" said Lance, with shining eyes. "I wonder what the next thing will be!"

"I feel a prophecy coming on," said Joel in a silly voice with a far away expression in his eyes. "It's for you, Lance! Your next task will be . . . science homework and tidying your bedroom! Well, actually," he admitted, after removing a well-aimed cushion from his face, "I overheard your mum!"